Where is C?

Tony Mitton

Illustrated by Jo Brooker

Photographed by Keith Lillis

RIGBY

The ladybird wanted to play.
"Where is Curly?
Where did he go?" she asked.

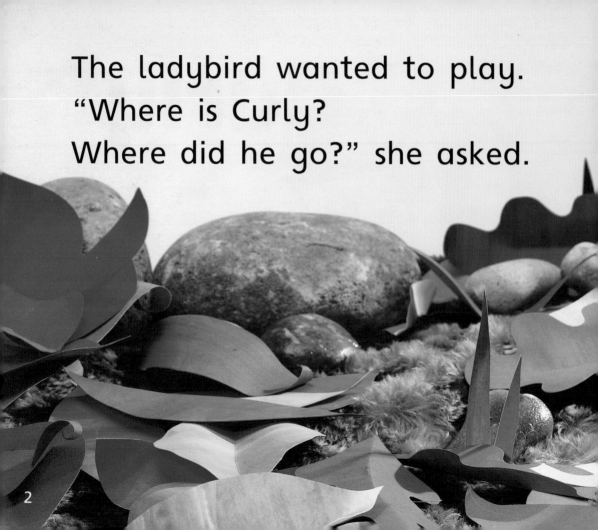

Along came the beetle.
"Where is Curly?" he asked.
"Is he under here?"

Along came the grasshopper.
"Where is Curly?" he asked.
"Is he up here?"

Along came the worm.
"Where is Curly?" he asked.
"He is not down here."

The snail came along.
"Where is Curly?" he asked.
"He is not under here."

"Where **is** Curly?"
asked the ladybird.
"He is not in here."

"We can't find Curly!"
said all his friends.